WRITTEN BY
Andrew Murray

ILLUSTRATED BY
Sarah Horne

ORCHARD BOOKS
338 Euston Road, London NW1 3BH
Orchard Books Australia
Level 17/207 Kent Street, Sydney, NSW 2000
First published in hardback in Great Britain in 2009 by Orchard Books
First published in paperback in 2009
ISBN 978 1 84616 349 4 (hardback)
ISBN 978 1 84616 358 6 (paperback)

A CIP catalogue record for this book is available from the British Library.
1 3 5 7 9 10 8 6 4 2 (hardback)
1 3 5 7 9 10 8 6 4 2 (paperback)
Printed in Great Britain
Orchard Books is a division of Hachette Children's Books,
an Hachette UK company.
www.hachette.co.uk

Charlie looked down at the glossy tour brochure.

A real haunted castle, with real ghosts? Charlie could hardly believe it.

"Mum," he said, "Dad, are the ghosts really real?"

"We'll soon find out, Charlie," they said.

Fairfax Castle was crowded with people buying ghostly souvenirs, eating ghostly snacks, and waiting for the next ghostly performance. One stand was selling raffle tickets, to win Fairfax Castle goodies, and Dad bought a ticket.

The Fairfax ghosts came out to perform on a stage in the Great Hall every hour. At noon, a happy crowd sat down, ready to be scared.

Charlie couldn't wait. "When are we going to see some ghosts?"

Huge curtains closed over the windows and the Great Hall was plunged into darkness. A tall thin woman with a gleaming white smile appeared on the stage, holding a candle.

"Ladies and gentlemen," she announced. "My name is Edwina Predder.

"Welcome to Fairfax Castle! Soon you will see the dead come alive! You will see the ghosts of Lord Reginald Fairfax, Lady Cynthia, their daughter Florence, and even their pets, Zanzibar the dog and Rio the parrot! You will see them – and you will never forget them!"

Edwina Predder left the stage, and the hall was dark and silent. Charlie chewed his fingernails.

In the darkness a wisp of smoky grey appeared. It wriggled and grew into the shape of a man – a handsome man with a long moustache. The crowd gasped.

"Lord Fairfax!" whispered Charlie. And for a moment Lord Fairfax looked straight at Charlie... His eyes were grey and deep, and seemed very old and faraway. But there was something else about those eyes, something that Charlie couldn't quite figure out.

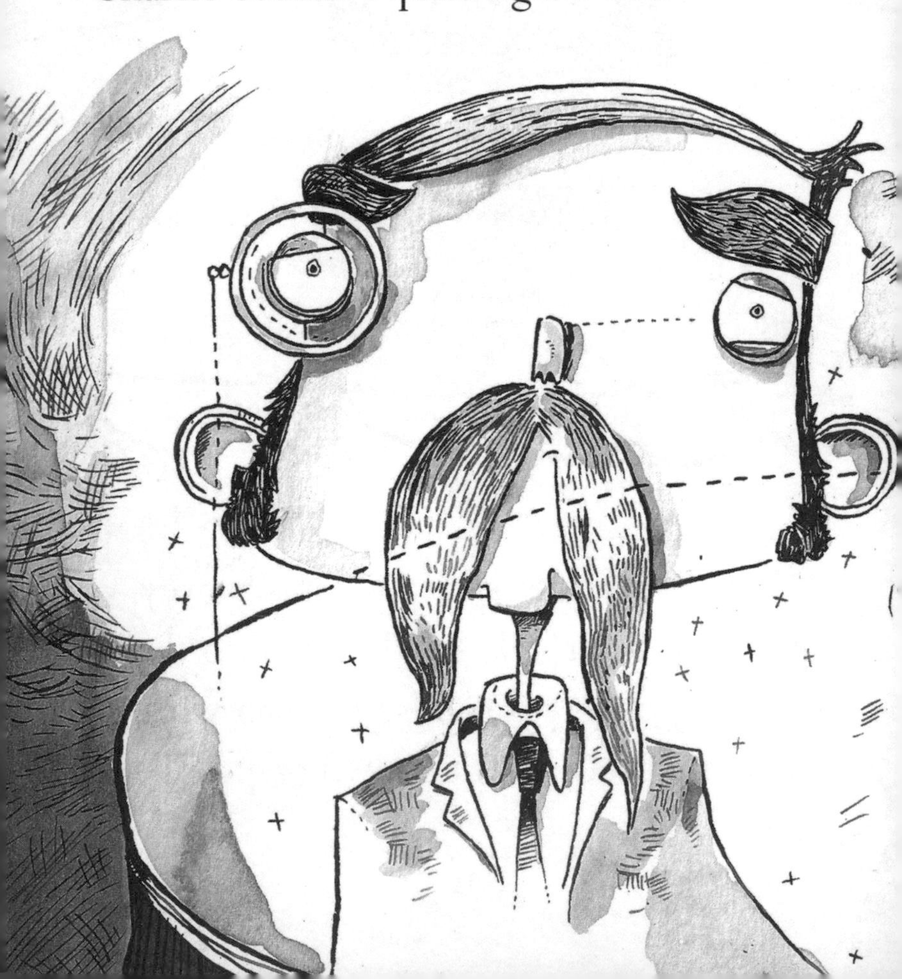

Then more wisps appeared, and wriggled and grew. They became Lady Cynthia, Florence, Zanzibar the dog and Rio the parrot. There they were, walking and waving, barking and flapping – but misty and ghostly grey. Charlie could see right through them.

"They're really ghosts!" gasped Charlie. "Not magic tricks. Not movie tricks. They're real!" The ghosts were real indeed. And they sang a ghostly song:

At the "YOU!", everyone jumped out of their seats! Then they clapped and cheered and whistled.

"Wonderful!" they cried. "We've never been so scared! Bravo!"

The ghosts floated across the stage and waved goodbye. But Charlie was curious. He was thinking about the moment when Lord Fairfax looked him in the eye.

He looked...sad, somehow, thought Charlie. *Yes, that's it, sad – as if he really doesn't enjoy doing all this.*

Charlie wandered off to look for the toilets. Fairfax Castle was huge, and empty. It was full of grand winding corridors and grand silent halls, lined with grand wood panels and decorated with grand paintings.

He was beginning to feel desperate for the toilet when he eventually saw the sign: GENTLEMEN.

As Charlie was washing his hands, he heard muffled noises coming from below, down some old, winding stairs that led into the Castle dungeons.

The stairs were slimy, and dark, and full of cobwebs. But Charlie was curious. He could feel his heart pounding in his chest – ba-doom, ba-doom, ba-doom! – as he crept down, step by step.

The darkness grew deeper and deeper the further he went, and soon Charlie couldn't see where to put his feet. He reached out with his toe, found the next step – and his foot slipped on the slime.

"Help!" He fell, and bumped, and bounced down several steps. "Ouch! Ouch! Owww!" He sat on the floor, feeling sore, listening to the echoes of his voice – "Ouch…ouch…ouu… ouuu…ooouuhhh…"

Charlie looked up. The faint light from the Castle seemed far away. Suddenly he felt very alone. His heart pounded even harder, and he could feel cold sweat on the palms of his hands and trickling down his back.

“Come on, Charlie!” he said to himself. “Don’t be silly, there’s nothing to be afraid of!” He brushed himself off and carried on down the stairs.

Soon Charlie couldn't even see his hand in front of his face. He stretched out his foot to feel below, and reached out his hand to feel ahead…

"Ugh!" He felt something silky, sticky and stringy. "Cobwebs – yuck!" In a panic, imagining huge hairy spiders dangling on his head and sitting on his shoulders, Charlie rushed down the stairs, until suddenly there was some light.

Trip, bump, clatter – "Ouch! Ouch! Owww!" Charlie stumbled and fell on the slimy stone floor.

He looked around. A faint, sickly yellow-green light shimmered on the crumbling stone walls.

This was very different from the Castle above. Instead of grand halls and paintings, it was a place of mouldy slime and rotten smells.

Then came the noises again – much louder and clearer now. They were voices, hissing voices, whispering voices. Charlie felt frozen with fear. His heart thumped in his ears so loudly that for a minute he could hear nothing else – ba-doom, ba-doom, ba-DOOM! He realised he had forgotten to breathe. Those voices – who were they?

Charlie had a sudden urge to rush back up the stairs, to light and people and safety. He scrabbled up the steps, crawling like a frightened animal, up and up and...

“Hang on!” he said suddenly to himself. “Charlie, stop for a minute! Calm down. Breathe...” And there he sat, panting, halfway between the voices below and the light above.

Half of him was afraid, but the other half was curious. The longer he sat there, the more he wanted to know who those voices belonged to.

"Come on, Charlie," he said. "If you go home now you'll always wonder who it was." And so, with cold sweat soaking his skin, he crept back down, into the yellow-green light, closer and closer to the voices.

Hissing, whispering, the voices were coming from just beyond an archway. Charlie took a deep breath, tried to feel big and brave, and peered round…

Before him was a stone cell, which someone had tried to smarten up with a carpet, some lights and a few ornaments. But all that Charlie noticed right then were the ghosts!

There they were, Lord and Lady Fairfax, their daughter Florence, Zanzibar the dog and Rio the parrot.

They were as wispy and see-through as before, but instead of laughing and singing, they all looked very unhappy.

Charlie crept a little closer so he could hear what they were saying.

"Edwina Predder is so horrible!" said Lord Fairfax.

"She treats us like slaves," agreed Lady Cynthia. "Every day, every hour, we have to perform for her, wave, smile, sing that silly song. I'm sick of it!"

"Can't we run away?" asked Florence. "Just run away from Fairfax Castle and find somewhere nicer to haunt?"

"Oh, Florence, my dear," sighed her father. "If only it were that easy. We're trapped here. We belong to the stones of Fairfax Castle, and the stones of the Castle hold us prisoner.

"We cannot get away. Believe me, Florence, I've tried, but when I got to the edge of the Castle grounds I ran into an invisible wall. Try as I might, I couldn't get any further."

Lord Fairfax sighed again. "There's the foundation stone," he said, pointing to a big stone set in the wall. "It's the very first stone that my great-ancestor, Rufus Fairfax, laid down when he began to build this Castle.

"If only we could make the stone fly far away – then perhaps we could fly away with it and be free. But we can't. We can't lift. We can't carry. We are ghosts, and we can't do anything!"

They all sighed, and Charlie looked at their sad, weary faces.

Poor ghosts! he thought. *How terrible to be a prisoner in your own home!* So he plucked up his courage, and stepped out of the shadows.

"Excuse me!" he said.

"What?" cried the ghosts. "Who's there? Who are you, boy?"

"I'm Charlie," said Charlie. "I couldn't help overhearing what you said. Maybe I could help you escape. That foundation stone would just fit in my bag. And I think I might be able to lift it. If we could cut the stone free somehow, then maybe I could carry it out of here."

"Cut the stone free?" snorted Lady Fairfax. "Impossible!"

"Wait a minute," said her husband. "Let's give the boy a chance. Hmm...it's an interesting idea, Charlie. But how are we going to cut the stone loose?"

"I know!" said Florence. "There's a big drill in the store room upstairs! I've seen it. It's got its own power generator and everything."

"Let's give it a try!" said Lord Fairfax.

Florence led them up the stone stairs to the store room. There, behind a stack of cardboard boxes, was the drill, attached to a great big orange generator.

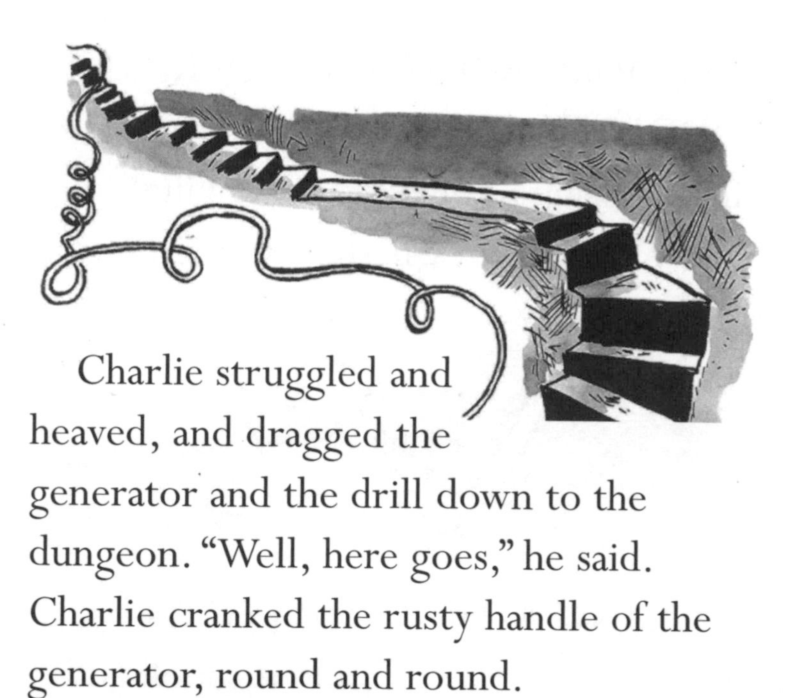

Charlie struggled and heaved, and dragged the generator and the drill down to the dungeon. "Well, here goes," he said. Charlie cranked the rusty handle of the generator, round and round.

"JUDDER-BUDDER-JUDDER-BUDDER!" The generator sprang into life, throwing out clouds of stinking blue smoke. Then Charlie switched on the drill.

"CLANG-A-TANG-A-BANG-A-JANG!" went the drill, and it shook and shuddered in Charlie's hands. With a great effort, he lifted it up and pointed it at the edge of the foundation stone.

"DZZZZZ-DZZ-DZZ-DZZZZZ!" the drill went as it bit into the stone. Phew, it was hard work! Clouds of dust rose up. Charlie's hands shook and shuddered, and soon got very sore. But he kept on drilling, drilling above and below and all around the stone.

Finally – just as he thought his arms were going to fall off and his hands were going to catch fire – the stone fell free, with a grinding thump, onto the floor.

"Brilliant!" clapped Florence.

"Well done, Charlie!" cried Lord Fairfax. Charlie found an old backpack in the store room, and now he took hold of the stone, and with a struggle, squeezed it into his bag. It was very, very heavy. Charlie staggered under the weight.

"Help!" he gasped.

"We'd love to help, Charlie," said the ghosts. "But all we can do is guide you."

So the ghosts led the way, and Charlie struggled along behind them. Up the stairs they went, along the corridors, towards the entrance of Fairfax Castle.

"We have to hide now, Charlie," said Lord Fairfax. "But we'll still be right here beside you, don't worry!" And although the ghosts faded away like mist in a morning breeze, Charlie could feel that they were still there.

They emerged into the Great Hall just as the one o'clock performance was about to begin. There was the crowd, watching excitedly in the darkness, and there was Edwina Predder, announcing the start of the show.

"Little does she know!" chuckled Charlie. "There's not going to be much of a show now!"

But then he slipped and his heavy, heavy load pulled him backwards. Crash! Charlie fell on the ground. A spotlight swept across him, and he could feel everyone looking at him.

"Goodness!" exclaimed Edwina Predder. "Young man, are you all right?"

"F-fine," said Charlie, trying to sound cheerful. "I just slipped." He struggled to get up.

"My, my!" said Edwina. "You seem to have something awfully heavy in that backpack."

Charlie froze. The ghosts froze. Did Edwina know? Had she guessed? Charlie could see what might happen now. Edwina would come over, open the pack and find the stone. Charlie would be arrested as a thief, and the ghosts would never escape.

The whole place was silent. Charlie's heart thumped in his chest. Then Edwina spoke.

"I hope you're not stealing the Fairfax family jewels!"

She laughed, and the whole crowd roared with laughter, too. Charlie breathed a deep sigh of relief. He struggled to his feet and hurried away from the show, to Mum and Dad, and to safety.

Outside, Charlie made his way to their car. He heaved the backpack into the boot.

"Charlie!" said Mum and Dad. "Where have you been?"

"I got lost," said Charlie. "Can we go now?" He looked anxiously over his shoulder. There was nobody there.

Are we going to get away with it? he wondered. *Are we going to get away with the stone?* Still, nobody had followed him.

"We've done it!" whispered Lord Fairfax.

"We're safe!" hissed Florence.

But just then a security guard came running towards them. "Stop!" he shouted.

"Oh no!" gasped Charlie. "Mum, Dad, let's go!"

"Stop!" yelled the guard. "Stoooooop!"

It was too late to escape. The guard was upon them. Charlie knew, and the Fairfaxes knew, that they had been caught.

"I've got you at last!" said the guard with a fierce grin. "You nearly got away – without your raffle prize!" And he held out the prize that Dad had won with his ticket. It was a Fairfax Castle paperweight.

"It's made of stone," smiled the guard. "Stone from Fairfax Castle."

"Stone from Fairfax Castle?" said Charlie. Here he was, stealing a stone, and now they were giving him another. It was too funny for words! Charlie grinned, then giggled, then laughed out loud – and he could feel the ghosts shaking with laughter beside him.

Charlie and his invisible friends squeezed into the back of the car. Dad drove out of the car park and down the driveway towards the main gates.

"This is it!" whispered Lord Fairfax in Charlie's ear. "We're about to leave Fairfax Castle. Now we'll see if the foundation stone does the trick. Hang on, everyone!"

Closer came the gates, closer and closer. The ghosts braced themselves, expecting to be yanked backwards by the magic of the Castle.

Dad drove through the gates...and nothing happened. Charlie could feel the ghosts beside him. They were still there.

"Are you all right?" whispered Charlie. "Is everyone all right?" And Charlie felt unseen hands patting him on the arms.

"Yes, Charlie!" they whispered. "It worked! Your plan worked! We're free! Free from her, for ever! Hip-hip-hurrah!"

Back home, Charlie buried the foundation stone so that it looked like just another rock in the garden. It seemed the Fairfaxes – and Zanzibar, and Rio – were here to stay.

Cool! thought Charlie. *I've always wanted to have a dog, and a parrot – and I don't even have to feed them or clean up their litter trays!*

Then Charlie turned to Lord Fairfax, who was sitting next to him in his bedroom, and said, "I wonder if there are other ghosts like you? Trapped in the places they haunt? Forced to perform for tourists? Or just annoyed by how annoying the living can be?"

Lord Fairfax puffed his cheeks. “I’ve never really thought about it,” he said. “Why not? You’re right, Charlie. Why shouldn’t there be other ghosts, suffering the way we used to suffer? But even if it is true, what can we do about it?”

“I’ve been thinking about that,” grinned Charlie, and he pointed at the computer screen.

"That?" said Lord Fairfax.

"That!" said Charlie. "What about a website? A website where ghosts can email us if they have any problems, if they're trapped, or pestered, or just plain upset? Then maybe we can go and rescue them? What do you think, Lord Fairfax?"

"I think that's a very, very good idea, Charlie! What are you going to call this website?"

"How about Ghost Rescue?"

And that's exactly what they did. Soon, a new website appeared on the internet.

And with that, Charlie and the ghosts sat back and waited for their first cry for help…

WRITTEN BY
Andrew Murray

ILLUSTRATED BY
Sarah Horne

Ghost Rescue	978 1 84616 349 4
Ghost Rescue and the Greedy Gorgonzolas	978 1 84616 350 0
Ghost Rescue and the Homesick Mummy	978 1 84616 352 4
Ghost Rescue and the Gloomy Ghost Train	978 1 84616 353 1
Ghost Rescue and the Horrible Hound	978 1 84616 354 8
Ghost Rescue and Mutterman's Zoo	978 1 84616 355 5
Ghost Rescue and the Dinosaurs	978 1 84616 356 2
Ghost Rescue and the Space Ghost	978 1 84616 357 9

All priced at £8.99

The Ghost Rescue books are available from all good bookshops,
or can be ordered direct from the publisher:
Orchard Books, PO BOX 29, Douglas IM99 1BQ
Credit card orders please telephone 01624 836000
or fax 01624 837033 or visit our website: www.orchardbooks.co.uk
or email: bookshop@enterprise.net for details.

To order please quote title, author and ISBN
and your full name and address.
Cheques and postal orders should be made payable to 'Bookpost plc'.
Postage and packing is FREE within the UK
(overseas customers should add £1.00 per book).

Prices and availability are subject to change.